The
Bedtime
Story

To: Emmy Zryniak

Sweet dreams
Little dreamer.

Smiles,
Lori

Illustrated by Christina Schofield

ISBN
978-1-77067-787-6 (Paperback)
978-1-77067-788-3 (eBook)

Produced by:

FriesenPress
Suite 300 — 852 Fort Street
Victoria, BC, Canada V8W 1H8

www.friesenpress.com

Distributed to the trade by The Ingram Book Company

This book is dedicated to my mother, Mary Lou, who loved to read. She chose my name from a character in one of her favorite books. From this memory, I created Tori.

This is Tori with her mommy and daddy in their family photo. Tori is four years old. She loves to play and have fun with all her toys. She has a great imagination. She has given all her toys names. Some of her special toys can talk to her. Tori can hear what they are saying, but her mommy and daddy cannot.

When Tori wakes up in the mornings she likes to play with her toys for a while before she goes and wakes up her mommy and daddy for breakfast. Yesterday, Mommy told Tori she could help her in the garden to plant some flowers. Tori likes helping her mommy and thought planting flowers would be fun. As Tori looked around her room, rubbing her eyes and yawning, she saw her doll Suzie.

"Oh, there you are, Suzie. Good morning," said Tori.

Suzie doll said, "Can I come outside and help plant flowers with you?"

"Of course you can, but we have to get dressed first," Tori said.

Tori put on her play clothes for outside and then dressed up Suzie. They both put on shorts, a T-shirt, and a hat because it was sunny and hot outside. Tori's shirt had a big sunflower on the front of it. *This is a perfect shirt to wear today*, she thought.

Tori and Suzie went downstairs for breakfast. They had cereal, toast, a banana, and a glass of milk. Tori decided to make a face with her breakfast. She used the crust from her toast for the eyebrows. She used some of her cereal for the eyes and the nose. Then she used her banana to make a big smile.

"That's a funny face," said Suzie.

Tori giggled and said, "It kind of looks like Daddy." Then she ate it all up.

"Are you ready to go outside now, Tori?" asked Mommy.

"Yes," said Tori.

Tori and Suzie helped plant lots of flowers in the garden with Mommy. After they put the flowers into the dirt, Tori's mommy said they had to water the flowers to help them grow. Tori got to use her own little watering can to water her flowers.

"Can I go play now?" asked Tori. "Suzie and I are tired of planting flowers."

Mommy thanked Tori for being such a good helper and told her she could go play, but to stay in the backyard.

"I will bring you a little picnic lunch to eat," Mommy said with a smile.

Tori was excited and ran to her playhouse. Daddy had built this playhouse for her. It had a big red slide on one side. Tori had forgotten something though. She forgot Suzie. Suzie was lying in the dirt in the garden.

Tori climbed inside her playhouse and found Patches, her giraffe, and Sprinkles, her kitty.

"There you are, Patches. I have been looking for you," said Tori. "What's that, Sprinkles?"

"Meow, meow," said Sprinkles.

"Okay, I hear you," said Tori.

"Let's have lunch. I'm hungry too. Then after lunch we will go down the slide," said Tori.

"Yeah!" said Patches. "I like going down the slide fast."

Tori giggled, "Me too, Patches."

The day went by quickly. Tori heard her mommy calling her.

"Tori, it's time to pick up your toys, come inside for supper, and have a bath," said Mommy. "It looks like it is going to rain soon."

Tori did not want to pick up her toys. She was having too much fun, so she continued to play.

The sun was almost gone behind the dark clouds. Soon Tori felt a few drops of rain on her head. Then she heard the crashing sound of thunder. Tori was scared and ran into the house, leaving all her toys outside.

After supper, her daddy asked her to pick up the toys she had left on the floor in the living room, but Tori did not pick up her toys.

Instead, she told her daddy, "I can't, I have to go have my bath now. Mommy is waiting for me." Then Tori ran up the stairs.

Tori was having fun in the bathtub playing with her toys. Then Mommy came in and washed her hair and helped her dry off with a big fluffy towel so she could go put on her nightgown and get ready for bed. Mommy told Tori she needed to pick up her toys in her bedroom and put them away inside her toy box after she got her nightgown on.

Tori did not pick up any of her toys, and when Mommy came into her room to tuck her into bed she was very sad to see the mess.

"What's wrong, Mommy?" asked Tori.

"Tori, I think it is time I told you a bedtime story that my mommy told me when I was your age," said Mommy. "The story is about a little boy named Ben and his toy soldiers."

Tori had already forgotten about the sad look on Mommy's face because she was excited to hear this new bedtime story.

Mommy sat in the rocking chair next to Tori's bed and began reading the story to her.

"Once upon a time, there was a little boy named Ben who loved to play with his toys. Every day Ben's mommy and daddy would ask Ben to pick up his toys and put them away, but Ben didn't like to pick up his toys because it was not fun."

"He's like me. I don't like picking up my toys either. It's not fun," Tori said, frowning.

"So," read Mommy, "Ben's toys were left out wherever he had played with them last. Many of his toys got stepped on and were broken. Ben had lots of puzzles, too, that he liked to put together and take apart, but because he had not put them away, some of the pieces had gotten lost."

"Ben also had a dog named Chester. Chester was a puppy and loved to chew on toys. Because Ben left his toys lying around, Chester would play with them and chew on them. Some of Ben's favorite toys were ruined. This made Ben very sad.

Ben's mommy decided to help him pick up all his toys. She told Ben that if he made picking up his toys into a game, it would be fun to do. She said his dump truck could help pick up all the toy blocks and dump them into the toy box. His crane could pick up his toy cars and drop them into the toy box.

This did sound like fun, Ben thought, so he started to help. Before long, all the toys were put away.

Afterwards, Ben saw that his mommy had put all the broken toys and the toys that were missing pieces into the garbage. When Ben saw this, he cried. He would miss playing with those toys."

"The next day Ben was outside in his backyard playing with his favorite toy soldiers. He pretended they were marching, like in a parade. Ben talked to his toy soldiers and gave them commands.

'Are the troops ready, Sergeant?' said Ben, who liked to pretend he was the captain.

'Yes, Captain,' said the sergeant soldier.

'Okay then, let's march. One, two, three, four,' said Ben. Then his toy soldiers marched across the top of the picnic table.

Ben then started flying his toy airplane. It was soaring through the air. He pretended some of his toy soldiers who had parachutes on were jumping out of the plane and flying through the air. They would land in the tall grass so they could hide from the bad guys.

Ben was having fun."

"Suppertime came, and Ben had to go inside the house."

"Do you think he remembered to pick up his toys?" Mommy asked Tori.

"I don't know," said Tori.

"No," said her mommy. "Ben did not pick up his toys, and to make things worse, it began to rain outside."

Mommy continued reading, "'Don't leave us, Ben!' the toy soldiers called out. 'We will be blown away with the wind,' yelled a soldier with a parachute on.

But Ben could not hear them because he had gone inside the house.

That night, after Ben went to sleep, the big rainstorm continued. By the morning it was over. When Ben woke up, he looked outside and saw his toy soldiers all on the ground.

'That is not where I left you,' Ben said looking puzzled.

The wind had blown his soldiers off the picnic table. They were lying in puddles on the ground. One soldier that had a parachute on had gotten caught on the fence when the wind tried to blow him away. The fence had ripped a big hole in the parachute.

'Oh no!' shouted Ben. 'Now he can't fly anymore.'"

"Ben's mommy saw what had happened. She asked Ben, 'If you were one of your toy soldiers, how would you feel right now?'

'They must think I don't care about them,' sighed Ben. Ben was sorry he had forgotten to put his toys away and left them outside in the bad weather. Then Ben realized Chester, their dog, was in the backyard.

'No, Chester! Stop!' yelled Ben. He saw Chester running to pick up one of his toy soldiers.

Ben's mommy came running and called Chester into the house."

Tori's mommy asked, "So what do you think happened with Ben and his toys?"

"Were his toys okay, Mommy?" asked Tori. "Oh, I hope they were okay," she said, looking very worried.

"Well, that is all the time we have for a bedtime story tonight, Tori. It is getting late," said Mommy.

"But what happened to Ben's toys?" asked Tori.

"I guess we won't know until tomorrow night when we finish the story," said Mommy. So Mommy tucked Tori in and gave her a kiss goodnight.

Tori wasn't sure she could go to sleep now because she wondered what was going to happen next to Ben and his toys. But all snug and warm in her bed, Tori did finally fall asleep until the loud tapping sound of rain hitting her window woke her up. She saw a bright flash of lightning. Then she heard the loud crashing noise of thunder. Tori was so frightened she jumped out of bed and ran down the hallway to Mommy and Daddy's bedroom.

"Can I sleep with you tonight?" Tori asked in a scared little voice.

"Of course you can," said Mommy.

"You will be safe here with us," said Daddy.

It was hard for Tori to fall asleep again with all the noise outside. She could see the rain through the window and could hear the strong wind howling, plus she could not stop thinking about the bedtime story her mommy had told her earlier. So Tori lay awake thinking about her day and all that had happened, until she finally fell asleep.

Once Tori was asleep, she began to dream. Tori dreamt she woke up and was cold and shivering. She tried to reach for the blankets to cover herself up, but she could not move her arms. She tried to sit up and move her legs, but she couldn't. Tori was scared, as she did not know what was happening.

Meanwhile outside, cold rain was falling onto Suzie doll's face, and mud was soaking into her clothes.

"Help!" shouted Suzie doll.

Suzie doll shouted as loud as she could for Mommy and Daddy to come help her, but she forgot they cannot hear her when she talks. So Suzie doll called out for Tori to come and save her, but Tori did not come either. Suzie began to cry and wondered if Tori did not love her anymore. Why did Tori leave me outside and not bring me into the house with her, Suzie wondered.

"What's going on? Where am I?" asked Tori.

Tori looked around and saw Suzie's hat lying beside her on the ground. She realized she was not in bed with her mommy and daddy anymore.

Suddenly, Tori realized she was not herself anymore. She had turned into her doll Suzie and was lying in the mud in the garden outside in the cold rain.

"If I am now my doll Suzie, who will look after me?" cried Tori.

Just then, Tori woke up. She looked around and realized it had all been a bad dream. It was early in the morning and she was still in bed with her mommy and daddy. She jumped up and ran to the window, looking outside for Suzie.

"I'm coming, Suzie!" shouted Tori.

Tori quickly ran to her bedroom and got dressed as fast as she could. Then she went downstairs and put on her raincoat, hat, and rubber boots. She went outside, found Suzie, and gave her the biggest hug ever.

"I do love you, Suzie. I love you very much," said Tori.

Tori found Patches, her giraffe, and Sprinkles, her kitty. She picked them up and told them how sorry she was that she had not taken better care of them. Tori brought all of her toys into the house.

Mommy helped fill the kitchen sink with some warm, soapy water. Tori gave all her toys a bath, which was fun. Then she put clean, dry clothes on Suzie so she would feel better.

"I promise I will never leave you outside again," said Tori.

Tori picked up all her toys in the living room and put them away. Then she went upstairs and picked up all her toys in her bedroom and put them away in her toy box. As she picked up her toys, she also played with them. Suzie, Patches, and Sprinkles, her best friends, helped Tori put all of her toys into the toy box.

Ben's mommy was right. Picking up your toys could be fun if you made it into a game.

That night when Mommy came into Tori's bedroom to tell her the rest of the bedtime story about Ben and his toy soldiers, Tori said she thought she might already know how the story ends. So Mommy let Tori finish telling the story.

"It is a happy ending," said Tori, smiling. "Ben picked up all of his toys, washed them, played with them, and put them away. I think Ben's mommy even sewed up the hole in the soldier's parachute so he could fly again. Ben learned how to take care of his toys because he loved them. So now, his toys will not get lost or broken and end up in the garbage. The end," said Tori.

Mommy said she liked how Tori finished telling the story. Tori said she liked stories with happy endings. Mommy kissed Tori goodnight and tucked her and Suzie into bed together under the nice, warm sheets.

"Sweet dreams," said Mommy as she turned out the lights and closed the door.

The End